# W*ILL
# AND
# S*QUI*LL

EMMA CHICHESTER CLARK

Andersen Press • London

For
Janice Thomson

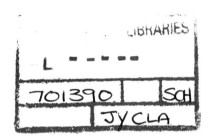

Copyright © 2005 by Emma Chichester Clark
The rights of Emma Chichester Clark to be identified as the author and illustrator
of this work have been asserted by her in accordance with the Copyright, Designs and Patents Act, 1988.
First published in Great Britain in 2005 by Andersen Press Ltd., 20 Vauxhall Bridge Road, London SW1V 2SA.
Published in Australia by Random House Australia Pty., 20 Alfred Street, Milsons Point, Sydney, NSW 2061.
All rights reserved. Colour separated in Switzerland by Photolitho AG, Zürich.
Printed and bound in Italy by Grafiche AZ, Verona.

10   9   8   7   6   5   4   3   2   1

British Library Cataloguing in Publication Data available.

ISBN 1 84270 382 X

This book has been printed on acid-free paper

This is how Will met Squill
and Squill met Will.
They were little.
Little Will and
Little Squill.

"Oh, my darling!"
cried Will's mother.

"Oh, my darling!"
cried Squill's
mother.

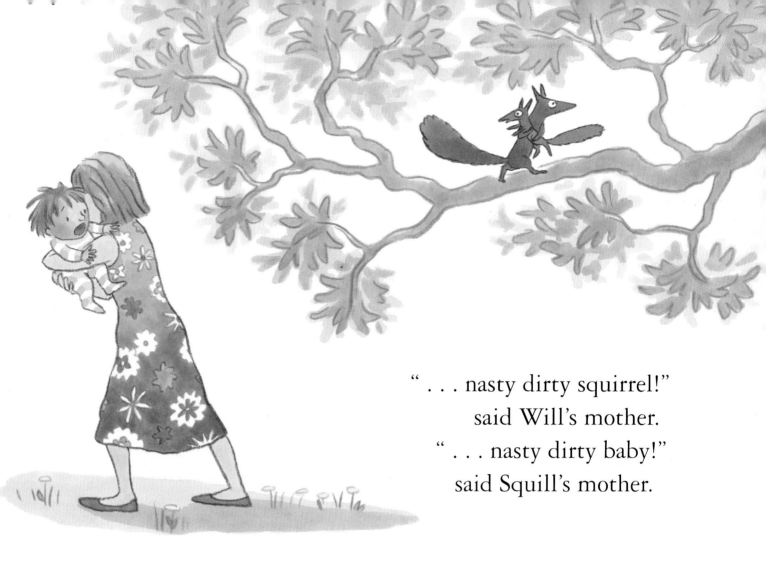

" . . . nasty dirty squirrel!"
said Will's mother.
" . . . nasty dirty baby!"
said Squill's mother.

But Squill wanted Will
and Will wanted Squill.

With Squill, Will
took his first steps.

With Will, Squill
had his first swim.

Squill grew. Will grew.

Will!

Squill!

Will's parents gave Will
lots of fluffy toys,
but he only wanted Squill.

Squill's parents gave Squill
lots of little brothers
and sisters, but
he only wanted Will.

They had plenty
of things to do.
"Swing!" said Squill.
"I will if you will!" said Will.
"I squill!" said Squill.

They had plenty of things to play.
"Squill will if Will will!" sang Squill.
"Will will if Squill will!" sang Will.

And they had plenty of things to try.
"Will you try some spaghetti, Squill?" asked Will.
"I will, Will," said Squill.
"I love squilletti!" said Squill.
"And wilkshake!" said Will.

They had the same bedtime,
in different places . . .

. . . but sometimes,
in the same place.

"Goodnight, Squill,"
said Will.
"Goodnight, Will,"
said Squill.

Then one day,
Will's parents
had a surprise
for Will.

"Oh!" cried Will.

"Your own little kitten!"
they said.
"Little kitty kitty!"
said Will.

"What a good little kitty,"
said Will.

"Look! She's dancing!"
said Will.

"Clever little kitty!"
said Will.

"Come on, kitty! Catch, little kitty!" said Will.
"Roly, poly, tickly tummy!" said Will.

"Silly little kitty!"
hissed Squill.

"Hey! Squill!"
cried Will.
"Stop that at once!"

"Poor little kitty!" said Will.
"Go away!" said Will.
"I will!" said Squill.

But . . . the kitten didn't really like bouncing.
And the kitten didn't really like football.

The kitten really didn't seem to want to do
anything . . . except sleep . . .

. . . and sleep.
The kitten wasn't
so much fun
after all.

Will missed Squill.
He missed everything about Squill.

"What's the matter, Will?"
asked his parents.
"I miss Squill," said Will.

"Where is Squill?
Will he ever come back?"
wondered Will.

And then,
Will saw Squill!

"Squill!" said Will.
"Will!" said Squill.
"You look silly!" said Will.
"I feel squilly!" said Squill.

"I really miss you, Squill," said Will.
"I really miss you, Will," said Squill.

"Will you say 'sorry'?"
asked Squill.
"I will if you will,"
said Will.
"I squill if you squill,"
said Squill.
"I'm sorry!" said Will.
"I'm sorry," said Squill.

"Well, I'm not sorry!"
cried the little girl.
"Can I play with your kitten?"

"Yes!" said Will.
"*Definitely* yes!"
said Squill.

"Dear little kitty!
Time for a little nap!"
said the little girl.
"*Yes!*" purred the kitten.

Squill's parents saw
and Will's parents saw
that where there's a Will
there's a Squill,
and where there's a Squill
there's a Will,
and it was better that way.

"I hope we'll always be friends," said Will.
"Squill will if Will will!" sang Squill.
"Will will if Squill will!" sang Will.
"So we will!" said Squill.
"Yes, we squill!" said Will.
And they were.
Forever.

THE END